MAYA & MIGUEL

TEACHER'S PET

Adapted by C. Tobin
Art Direction by Rick DeMonico
Designed by Heather Barber

No part of this publication may be reproduced, or stored in a retrieval system, or transmitted in any form or by any means, electronic, mechanical, photocopying, recording, or otherwise, without written permission of the publisher. For information regarding permission, write to Scholastic Inc., Attention: Permissions Department, 557 Broadway, New York, NY 10012.
ISBN 0-439-73385-5

12 11 10 9 8 7 6 5 4 3 2 1   5 6 7 8 9/10

Printed in the U.S.A.
First printing, Sepember 2005

SCHOLASTIC INC.

NEW YORK   TORONTO   LONDON   AUCKLAND   SYDNEY
MEXICO CITY   NEW DELHI   HONG KONG   BUENOS AIRES

The Santos family returns home at the end of a long day. . . .
ZZZZZZ
. . . and then Andy passed the ball to me, and GOOOOOAAAAAAAL! You should've seen me. I rocked!
That's wonderful, Miguelito! And how did you do on your math quiz? Did you "rock"?

Parrots are social animals. He considers you his flock — his family.
If you're gone all day, it could be he's a little lonely.
Sí.
GASP!
I knew something was wrong. Thank you so much, Dr. DasGupta.

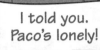

I told you. Paco's lonely!

We have been out a lot lately. I volunteer to stay home from now on and keep Paco company.

Don't be a clown, Miguel. We have to figure out a way to keep Paco from being lonely. But we have to go to school all day, and Mamá and Papi have to go to work, so . . .

BANG!

WHIZ!

POP!

¡Eso es! We'll take Paco to school with us!

We can't take Paco to school. He's a pet.
I can't believe you just said that in front of Paco. He's part of our flock! Our family! He's a Santos!
Okay, okay . . . he's family. But you can't just walk into school with Paco on your shoulder like you're a pirate.
Ahoy, mateys!
Although that would be pretty cool . . .
OUT of our way!
Or maybe not . . .

Well . . . you know Papi has those pet travel cases in his shop. I could make one of those into a backpack. That way I could carry Paco with me everywhere!

YAHOO! SQUAWK!

Later that Morning in History Class . . .
All right, class, I hope you read the Civil War chapter. Who can tell me who issued the Emancipation Proclamation?
Maya?
¡Quiero hablar!
I want to talk!

Great! Talk. Tell us the answer.
I ROCK! GOOOOAAAAAAAL!
AAARGGH!!!
Perhaps someone else would like to answer the question?

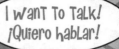

I want to talk! ¡Quiero hablar!

Go ahead. I'm all ears.

Um . . . I'm sorry, I meant to say that I DON'T want to talk but I was in such a hurry that I forgot to say "don't."

Oh. I see. Well, if you ever DO need to talk, please come see me.

Uh, yes sir. Thanks, Mr. Nguyen.

SQUAWK!

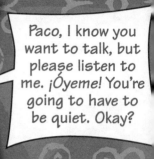

Paco, I know you want to talk, but please listen to me. ¡Óyeme! You're going to have to be quiet. Okay?

Cállate.

Sí. Be quiet.

Excuse me, may I get into my locker? I have class —

I noticed you were favoring your right leg a little, so I think you should sit out practice tomorrow until you're better.
OH, NO!
You don't have to take it so hard. It's not the end of the world. It's only until —

I'm sorry, Miguel! I left him on the bench during soccer and he got away. You have to help me find him.
You can count on me, Maya.
And me. Paco's part of my flock, too.
Oh, thanks guys! Now how will we find him?

We use what we know. Elementary deduction. First put yourself in Paco's shoes.
Paco doesn't wear shoes.
If you were a bird, where would you go?
The arcade!

No, Miguel, not where would *you* go, where would *Paco* go? Putting yourself in Paco's place means you're supposed to pretend you're Paco to try and understand his actions! *Be* Paco.

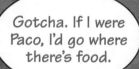

Gotcha. If I were Paco, I'd go where there's food.

Right. What does a parrot eat?

If you know the answer Theo, just tell us!
Oh, all right. The science class greenhouse.
BUT WHERE COULD PACO BE HIDING?
I don't see him anywhere.

MEANWHILE, MAYA FOLLOWS
THE SUNFLOWER SEED TRAIL . . .

Are you okay, Maya?

If you're hungry, they're serving Cornish game hen today.

C-cornish game hen?

Yes, it's like a chicken. A really small chicken.
Cornish game hen! Ha-ha! Thank you!
Er . . . You're welcome, Maya.
Maya, come quick! Theo thinks he's found a lead to Paco!

While Miguel is distracting Mr. Nguyen, we need to search every nook and cranny, every closet . . .

. . . for anything that squawks. Listen carefully for Paco's calls.

Then what do we do?
If you see a parrot, lure it with these sunflower seeds. They won't be able to resist.

MEANWHILE, MIGUEL IS STILL STROLLING WITH MR. NGUYEN. . . .
How will I ever remember all those important dates in history? I mean, there are so many of them. I can't keep them all straight!
I'd love to talk about this more, Miguel, but I have a class in a few min —
Paquito! It's me, Maya! I have sunflower seeds for you! PAQUITO!
Is that — ?

Don't you want to talk about history some more?
Not right now.
Maya, what's going on? What is my parrot doing up there?
Mr. Nguyen, it's all my fault. I set your parrot loose by accident. The other parrot is Paco.

He's part of my flock. My family. He was lonely and sad, so I thought I should bring him to school to make him happy. But he got away, and when I was looking for him . . .

. . . your parrot got out, too. I'm so sorry, Mr. Nguyen.

A lot of things are starting to make sense now. But you could have just told me, you know. I wouldn't have been mad.

You wouldn't?

Of course not. I bring my parrot, Minh, to school because I'm worried she's lonely and sad, too. But I spend so much time working.
She obviously needed more companionship.
Maybe Minh and Paco need a bigger flock.
If she says "eso es," run!

Did you read chapter four?
Of course I did.
Esperen, muchachos. Aren't you forgetting something?
Gracias, Mamá.

THE END